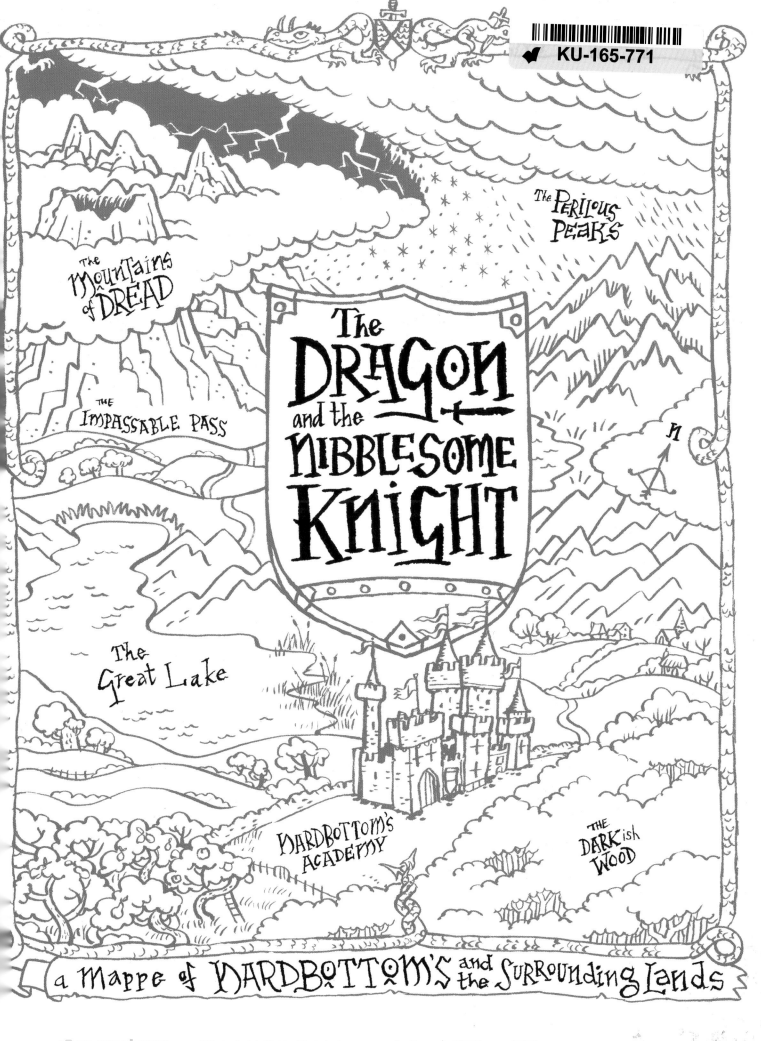

The PERILOUS PEAKS

The MOUNTAINS of DREAD

THE IMPASSABLE PASS

The DRAGON and the NIBBLESOME KNIGHT

The Great Lake

HARDBOTTOM'S ACADEMY

THE DARKish WOOD

a Mappe of HARDBOTTOM'S and the SURROUNDING Lands

SIG: 1 - A - Int_V1_HardBack_Ingles ... the Dragon and Nibblesome_27026

PROF. HARDBOTTOM'S ACADEMY FOR YOUNG KNIGHTS

SCHOOL SPORTS DAY!
FIGHT A REAL LIVE DRAGON!
TOMORROW

For the Extremely Fantastic
Emily Ford, with thanks
E.W.

For Eleano
B.D.

First published 2016 by Macmillan Children's Boo
an imprint of Pan Macmillan, 20 New Wharf Road, London N1 9R
Associated companies throughout the world. www.panmacmillan.co
ISBN: 978-1-4472-5480-5 (HB), ISBN: 978-1-4472-5481-2 (P.
Printed in Spain   9 8 7 6 5 4 3 2

ELLI
WOOLLARD

BENJI
DAVIES

The DRAGON and the NIBBLESOME KNIGHT

MACMILLAN CHILDREN'S BOOKS

The Dragons of Dread were a terrible bunch!
They ate boys for their breakfast and girls for their lunch.
But their best things of all, their favourite delights
were dribblesome, nibblesome, knobble-kneed knights.

When the smallest of all of the dragons turned four
his parents said, "Dram, you're a baby no more!
This nest's getting cramped and you've never once flown.
Now go bite a nibblesome knight of your own!"

So Dram stretched his wings and he started to flap.

But the lightening went FLASH!

and the thunder went CLAP!

It hailed and it galed and the winds looped and curled.

And they whisked Dram away to the End of the World

Where he thumped and he bumped
and went bounce, clatter, CRASH!

And he fell in a lake
with a fountainous . . .

SPLASH!

Now watching the skies by the edge of the shore
was young James, who had not seen a dragon before.
And he cried, "What was that? It's some rare kind of duck!
It seems to be hurt! What to do? What bad luck!"

So he took off his armour and said with a grin,

"I'm coming to help you!" And he waded right in.

"A lad?" muttered Dram. "Well, he might taste alright.
Though my Mum said I must nab a nibblesome knight."
And he stretched out a claw, then he suddenly stopped.
His leg was all bent and his paw simply flopped.

"Oh duckie!" cried James. "Why, you poor injured thing!
Sit yourself down and I'll make you a sling."

That's better! thought Dram. Now I must find a bite
of a dribblesome, nibblesome, knobble-kneed knight.
So he waved a goodbye and he tried to breathe smoke
but all that came out was a hoarse kind of croak.

"Oh duckie!" cried James, as Dram struggled to roar.

"What a strange sort of quack! Why, your throat must be sore!

Come to the woods and I'll fetch you some honey.

It makes a good medicine, all soothing and runny."

That's better! thought Dram. Now I must find a bite
of a dribblesome, nibblesome, knobble-kneed knight.
So he waved a goodbye and he started to fly
but his wings were too weak to take off in the sky.

"Oh duckie!" cried James. "I'm so dreadfully rude!

You must feel quite faint, let me get you some food.

Come to the orchard, we'll soon fill our tums

full of pears and pink peaches and big purple plums."

"That's better," yawned Dram.
"Now I must find a bite..."
But he fell fast asleep
in the moon-marbled night.

In the morning Dram woke and said, "Hey, I feel fine!
Soon a bite of a nibblesome knight will be mine!"
And he bellowed out billions of billowing flames
then he thought, I'll say bye to that little lad James.

TODAY:
SCHOOL
SPORTS
DAY!
WITH
SPECIAL GUESTS
THE DRAGONS OF DREAD

So he strode down the road
and he stomped through the field . . .

. . . and there was young James
with a sword and a shield!

SP

"You're a knight?" shouted Dram.
"You're not simply a lad?"

"You're a dragon?" yelled James.
"You're all beastly and bad?"

"Yes," muttered Dram.

"I suppose I should bite."

"Oh!" mumbled James.

"Then I guess I should fight . . .

. . . it must be all over. The finish.

The end!"

Then they both said at once, "But I can't,
YOU'RE MY FRIEND!"

"My friend!" chortled James,
as he put down his sword.

"My friend!" shouted Dram
and he smiled as he roared.

The knights all said, "Dragons, they're not simply beasts."
The dragons said, "Knights aren't so nice for our feasts.

Nibble at knights? Why, of course we do not!"

Though every so often, they sort of . . .

. . . forgot.